For Farzi Moussavi, with love ~ S.R.

For Linus ~ H.L.

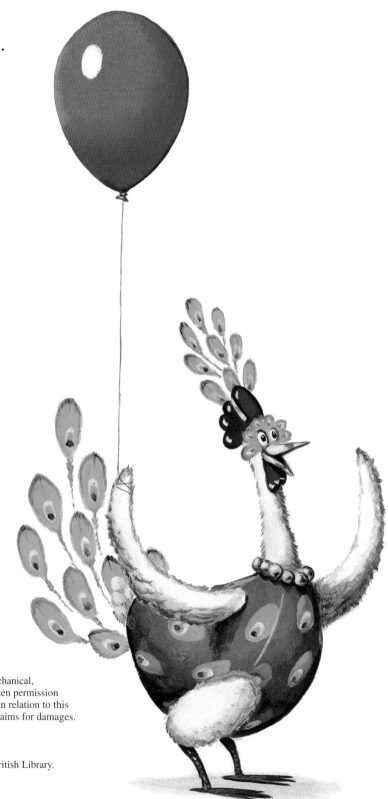

First published in 2006 by Macmillan Children's Books
a division of Macmillan Publishers Limited
20 New Wharf Road, London N1 9RR
Basingstoke and Oxford
Associated companies worldwide
www.panmacmillan.com

ISBN 1 405 02208 6 (HB)
ISBN 1 405 02209 4 (PB)

Text copyright © 2006 Shen Roddie
Illustrations copyright © 2006 Henning Löhlein
Moral rights asserted

9 8 7 6 5 4 3 2 1

A CIP catalogue record for this book is available from the British Library.

Printed in Belgium by Proost

CR
P
ROD

MY NAME IS
Mr Fox

Written by
Shen Roddie

Illustrated by
Henning Löhlein

MACMILLAN CHILDREN'S BOOKS

The hens were flapping
with excitement!
It was the morning of
the Fancy Dress Ball.

"I'm going as Peacock!" squealed Lou.
"Pea-brained idea, my dear," said Speck. "I'm going
in a disguise that's sure to win first prize!"
"What kind of disguise?" asked Lou.
"Never you mind," answered Speck, rudely.

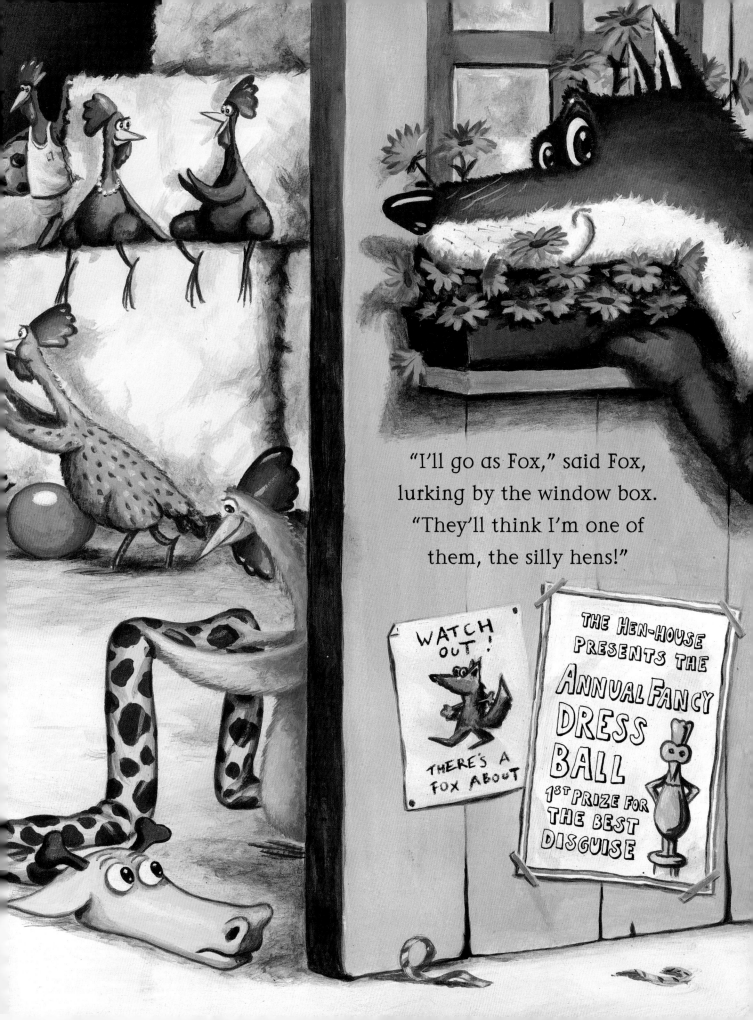

"I'll go as Fox," said Fox,
lurking by the window box.
"They'll think I'm one of
them, the silly hens!"

WATCH
OUT!

THERE'S A
FOX ABOUT

THE HEN-HOUSE
PRESENTS THE
ANNUAL FANCY
DRESS
BALL
1ST PRIZE FOR
THE BEST
DISGUISE

That evening,
Fox brushed his
bushy tail . . .

fixed on a
bow tie . . .

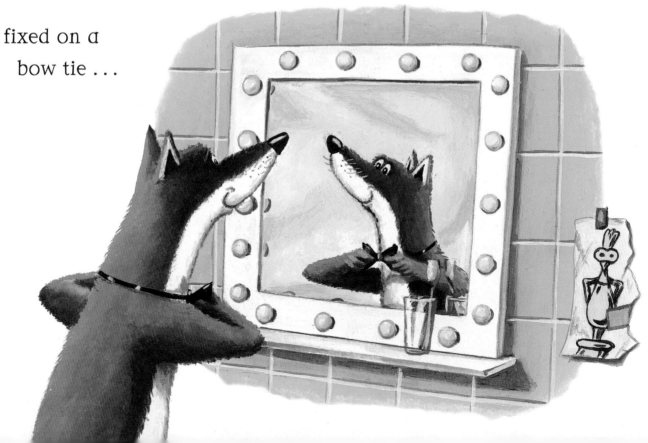

...and strode out into the moonlight.

"You handsome devil," he muttered to himself.

The ball began.
Speck, disguised as The Great Detective,
was about to dance with Lou when Fox cut in.

"May I?" asked Fox,
his whiskers bristling.
Lou blushed.

They danced cheek to beak.
"You look good enough to eat," said Fox, licking his lips.
"And you look like you COULD eat me!"
laughed Lou. "What a great disguise!"
"Tell me," she whispered, "are you Speck?"

"No. My name
is Mr Fox,"
said Fox.

"Ha! Ha! Ha! You
rascally rooster!"
laughed Lou.

"Don't you believe me?" said Fox. "Watch this!"
He howled.

HAWOOO!

"Brilliant!" screamed Lou, her feathers rising.

He bared his teeth.

GRRR!

"Scary!" yelled the hens,
diving for cover.

"Cluckitty-ha-ha!" laughed the hens.

"You're wonderful!" whispered Lou. "Who made your costume?"
"My mum," said Fox.
"Lucky you!" said Lou. "I had to make mine. Now be
a sweetcorn and own up. Are you Speck?"

"No, I'm HUNGRY FOX!" said Fox.
"And I'm Starving Peacock," giggled Lou.
"Then how about some chicken – I mean,
cherry – pie?" said Fox. "I know just the place."

So off they ran,
across the field.

Suddenly Lou
stumbled and both
of them tumbled.

"WHOOPSIE!"
squealed Lou, when
six peacock feathers
went flying.

Then, "WHOOPSIE POOPSIE!"
when her buttons popped off.

"Oh dear!" she wailed.
"Now you know who I am!
But why hasn't YOUR
costume come undone?"

"Because there are no buttons,
fluffhead," said Fox.

"A costume
with no buttons?
How very odd!"
thought Speck.

They arrived at Fox's house.

"But there's no pie,"
said Lou, looking round.

"Then we'll make one,"
said Fox.

Just then, they heard over the clear night air . . .

"Ladies and gentlemen, the winner of tonight's Fancy Dress Ball is ..."

"... MR FOX!"

"YOU'VE WON!" cried Lou.
"First Prize for the Best Disguise! Now you MUST tell me who you are!"

"I will if you get into the pot quick!" said Fox.
"Then we can collect the prize together,
as Fox and his Peacock Pie!"

"Stunning," giggled Lou, as she climbed into the pot.

Fox slapped the pie crust down. But just as he was
about to turn on the oven, the door burst open.
In ran Speck and the three judges, with
the other hens following behind.

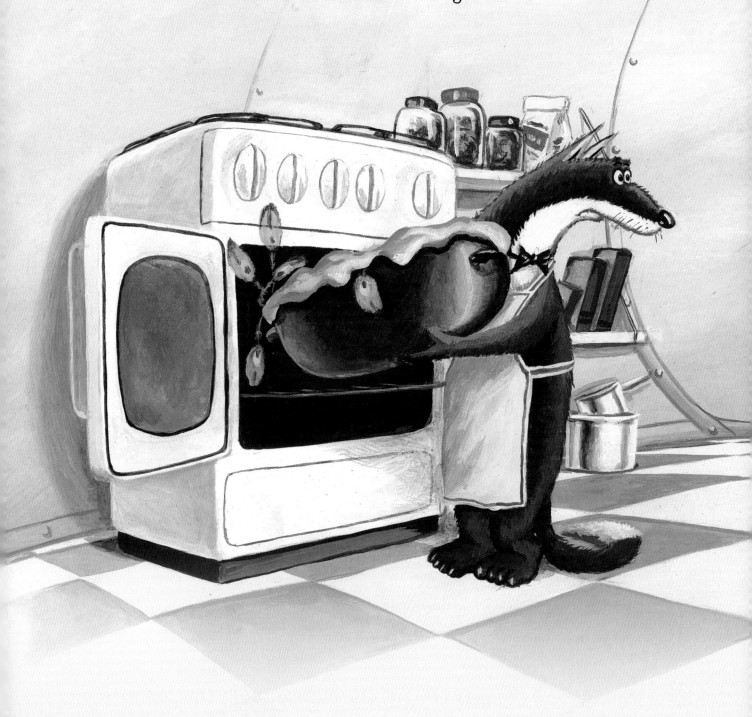

"FIRST PRIZE FOR THE BEST DISGUISE!"
announced the judges.

"But first, Mr Fox," said Speck,
"let me help you out of your costume."

Fox took one look
at the scissors . . .

and jumped straight out of
the window with Speck, the
Great Detective, hot on his heels . . .

just as Lou
popped out of the pot.

"Fancy running off like that – without
even a thank you!" said the judges.

"It MUST have been Speck," said Lou.
"He never did have good manners!"

"But what an AMAZING actor!
My name is Mr Fox indeed!" the hens said,
as they laughed, cluckitty-ha-ha,
all the way back to the ball.